MW01441721

CALL HIM BLACK

Prepubescent Stories from a Quaint Village

Blackfite Communications
Kingston, Jamaica WI

Also by Napoleon Black
When He Ascended
The Crucified Life
Light Afflictions
Fighting Lightning
"If" Moments with God

Copyright© 2024

ISBN 9798392740543
ALL RIGHTS RESERVED

Without limiting the rights under copyright reserved above, no part of this publication may be reproduced, stored in, or introduced into any retrieval system or transmitted, in any form or by any means (electronic, mechanical, photocopying, recording, or otherwise) without the prior contractual or written permission of the copyright owner of this work.

Editor: Robert Green

Cover Designer: Robert Green

Layout: Robert Green

Published by
Blackfite Communications
100 ¼ Molynes Road, Kingston 20, St. Andrew
Kingston, Jamaica
Gmail: Blackfite9@gmail.com
X: @blackfite_nb

Dedicated to
Eric and Erica, Precious, Richard, Bobbette,
and Beauty

ENDORSEMENTS

An enthralling, gripping form of storytelling. It bears a delineated tale of unbearable sadness but embraces hope and a determination to rise above and stand tall. Poems are filled with heartbreak, but very irresistible and gripping. Honest, raw, insightful, a must-read.

Sir Napoleon, you have entrenched yourself in the folds of great poets and have crafted a gripping anthology of poems.

Coleen Michelle Taylor
Teacher at Dunrobin Primary School

Thanks for allowing me the privilege of hearing your heartbeat and touching the edges of your soul, as you recounted your journey from childhood in family and in community.

This autobiographical work packaged in the lines of this anthology of poems, probes the mind of an innocent boy, stripped of innocence by the facts of his reality, forcing the strait-laced mind to bend, bob, and weave to the rhythms of his experiences. It is amazing how the sights, smells, tastes, and sounds that one may have never experienced, can be felt through the lines and stanza. The musing, reflections, memories, meandering, and wondering convulse on the canvas of the mind, as they jump from pages of the author's life.

I am cringing, I am laughing, I am

sympathizing, I am being disgusted and yet encouraged – as I rolled back your curtains of memories, and peeked into the stew of many curves and turns in that little village in the belly of a sugar estate, lined by the beauty of the avenue of bamboos, all of which natured and made you, you, uniquely – Black.

Tanneice Ellis
Carimac UWI

    This book is highly recommended. Oftentimes childhood books and books about childhood experiences are happy ones. Napoleon described his childhood as a grim one. I found the experiences mentioned real to the core. Through reading, themes such as Afrocentric religious practices, abandonment, neglect, abuse, loneliness, and belonging emerged.
    All credit to his teacher. She accepted him. She gave him hope. Perhaps that hope made him the man he is today; humble and a success. We all can attest to a person who showed up in our lives to show unconditional love or attention so that we could become the men and women we are today. In conclusion, Napoleon's story though it may be bleak, challenges others to share their stories and causes one to introspect on how it has shaped their personality. Usually, strong personalities are created through experiences like these, though unwanted.

Marcelee Kenion
Teacher, Greenpond High School

FOREWORD BY YANIQUE ROSS

My father has always been great with words; spoken words, written words, silent words, it did not matter. I have always thought it was genius the way he could make the words connect to people on all levels. Whether you were well taught, a little less taught, or thought that being taught was only for the taught, the words would matter and illuminate.

Growing up I would assume by his love for the use of his small black camera that he would take up photography, however, it wasn't the love of photography that would illuminate the minds of those he came in contact with it was his words.

This book of poetry addresses the most important issues in our lives: love, sorrow, belief, and identity. My father embarks on this voyage and paints such a masterpiece. Poetry's significance extends beyond its role in conserving culture and legacy. Many generations used poetry to document their history, beliefs, and experiences.

My father's poetry gives a window into his world, giving us his loved ones and future generations a unique perspective in his past. This collection of poems captures the spirit of a beautiful time lived by him.

In this volume, he preserves communal memories while providing a voice to people who would otherwise be forgotten. As you read may the words wrap you, comfort you, and illuminate the darkness wherever it may be found.

INTRODUCTION

Many have an opportunity to tell of their early formation. And I believe that all our stories add to the tapestry of our humanness. Here, I use real-life stories of my formative years to add that tapestry and infuse them with imagination to give them some colour. They represent some of my memories as a child growing up in Holland Village, a little settlement in North West St. Elizabeth, Jamaica.

We grew up in a time when electricity had not yet come to our village, and the roads were still marl. It was rich in greenery and untouched by cold lifeless modernization. The village had none of the features of contemporary life.

The first time the Village was introduced to electricity was when Maas Lanny and Aunty Imo came to live in our village. Aunty Imo was returning home, and she was accompanied by her husband. They brought with them, a Delco plant that Maas Lanny set up and which he would rev up in the evenings to light his house and his shop.

For sure, there was electricity on the Sugar Estate, and at Holland Primary School, but there was none in the Village. As children, we grew up in the innocence and rawness of our obliviousness. We roamed practically naked as boys.

We didn't know what hunger was, for some fruit was always in season, mangoes, cashews, June plum (I later learned it was also called Dew Plum), guava, cherry, gimbillings, custard apple, star apple, hog berry, bananas, coconut, ebbe, and of course sugar cane. And everybody planted something, Renta, Mozzela, St. Vincent, Yellow Yam, Coco, Dasheen, Baddoe, Bitter and Sweet Cassavas, gungo peas, peanuts, and our village was littered with mango trees, breadfruit trees, and other fruit trees.

We grew up under the stars, and the moon always seemed extra close to us. We sang and played all kinds of games and our parents told us stories of Anansy and Tacoma, of Rolling Calves, and an assortment of duppies. Mama Elsie who was born in 1886, our great-grandmother, would tell us stories of the Great Kaiser War, which I learned at Munro College was in fact World War 1. We looked at Mama Elsie with open-eyed wonder as she told us these stories.

At late evenings or early nights, we bathed outside in our moms' wash pans, or in one of the canals on the Estate where we would also catch fish and shrimps, or at the Big Pipe just outside of the mysterious Shaws Great House, where Uncle Barrows, Mama Enid's common-law husband, worked.

We grew up with simple things, and simple toys of our own making – catapults, push carts, gigs, and various means of transport. and no one thought of themselves as poor. When we had to travel from out of our village down to Miss Sivie's shop or further down to Shaws, at the Western end of Bambo Avenue to catch drinking water. Sometimes some of us got a ride on Jennet, Uncle Rawshut's donkey, a most uncomfortable, but joyful experience.

We didn't know what it meant to be poor. The word was never a part of our vocabulary. We only knew that people on the estate side lived in bigger and better houses, and had electricity, and some students from that side were dropped off at Holland Primary School in estate-owned vehicles. Most of the children from the Estate side too, seemed to speak a different language from us from Village, but we understood each other well enough. Despite the challenges of our village, we were generally happy as children as we had a sense of belonging there.

The stories captured here paint a picture of the tension between hope and loss, between the fierceness of village life and the inner hunger for more. It is the story of chaos and order, paradoxes, and plain sense, dreaming and reality.

Also, they tell the story of real people trying to make sense of a village that locked them in by its own mystique, and which seemed a closed system, its grip unyielding. Even if you left, you seemed bound to come back.

In a special sense, the story of the village is also the story of people who dared to break through the village's quaintness to make their mark too. It is an outsider who enters the village and imparts life to the poet. His Primary School teacher Miss Beckford offered him hope. Most people who attended Holland United church lived outside of the community but added to the richness of Village life.

Sickness and death scream from the pages of the work, creating a morbidity, rivalled only by the desire to celebrate and to dream, and to dance between the raindrops. Death is broken by a tenancy to live, to resist the opinion of the doctor, to fight through the graveyard back to the clearing and that tenacity was sharpened even when living meant submitting to the patriarchal social structure.

It tells the tale too of a mother, the ward of the state, and how her journey to give love to a child and his siblings shaped her passions. She was caught in the space of creating meaning and purpose for her children, as she mothered her children through a tough journey. Her ultimate hope was that her son and her other children would break the cycle and transcend the shackles of the village.

It tells of the power of cultural retentions at the crossroads and its latent malevolence. It tells how African retentions played a critical role in dealing with sickness and in the treatment of the sick, how those retentions impacted celebration in the community, and how easily culture became the ultimate cloak of identity.

It is the dreams and imaginings of the poet though that define the stories beyond anything else. These offered him something he knew was beyond the walls of the village. His dancing in the rain, His dream, his intense loneliness, and even his interpretation of his mother's harshness, all shaped him into being proud and … yes

Black.

TABLE OF CONTENTS

The Meeting
Call Him Black
A Visit to the Doctor
Death at First Sight
The Woman Who Warns
Gumbeh
Unwanted
Fed
Upside-Down Love
Lice
Dream
Hands Up
First Meeting
When it Rains
First Love
Zion
Sick Again
Fight
Beating
Bamboo Avenue
Lost in the Cemetery
Four Roads
Ode to Miss Beckford
Burning Cane
Pinky Pond
Christmas Morning

THE MEETING

A slip of a girl, breasts barely formed
Seduced by her own pain to love the enigmatic
dark rider.
His bike roars along the dirt track of the
primeval village,
Drenched in its own fear and anger and mystique
Wet with its peculiar drunkenness, desiring
to be discovered,
To be known, to be felt, to be touched.
Like an eagle announcing his majestic presence,
he comes
Her heart dances at the sound, for her courtesan
has come.
Girls giggle their rabid jealousy that she is favoured
And like wings, a tormenting tasteful current
lifts her to him
Seats her with him, by him, as he roars his Triumph
Dust encircles them like incense enfolds deity
in the Parthenon
And in the incandescence of splendor,
they are gone.
The village sighs, and trees rest their branches on
their cheeks, watching nothing
Birds flutter disturbed, distressed, distrait,
disquieted
The dust settles in eerie silence like a falling
feathered thud
And all is well again.

CALL HIM BLACK

I was born black, very black,
Like Dunder Hole refuse from making sugar
At the Sugar Estate factory,
Its refuse enveloped in stench,
Nothing desirable, but a repugnant decour
Bathed, but not clean
Instinctive, breathing with sides pulsating loss.
Wrapped but raw in my dizzying nakedness.
I was born black, very black,
Crying in the dark caverns of an empty life
Hope sucked in that first slap by Mama Elsie
A boy, strange, unresponsive, silent
No sound but the dark drag of Tuesday's light
The universe chortled a cynical lullaby
For no song would soothe the hunger of the shapeless heart
Beating a harsh tormenting non-rhythm
I was born black, Napoleon Black

A VISIT TO THE DOCTOR

Veins curdle in death as their spasms decrepitate a tired body
Fevered in the chilliness of the callous office
Weakened by the assailing darkness of a long wait.
Mother holds on to the mere skeletal frame
Watching parted lips dried like cinders from an empty fireside
And sunken waterless cheesy eyes already digging a grave
Tenuous in hope like a slender wisp pulling a giant coffin
 As every laboured breath heightens the tension
 Fearing fear, imagining that that was the last breath
But hoping hopefully that the last breath would make way for the next.
She grabs vehemently onto the coffin of bones, willing it to live
Fever fire maddening the moment
Tight squeezing… no… holding hard
That the frame in her calloused hopeful hands would keep on breathing.
The doctor stands and pronounces death.
As empty eyes dig deep in her soul
"It's going to die," …
A deep, unconcerned, detached, as a matter-of-fact disconnect
Placing a hard thumb on the bedraggled coffin of his body

Pulling back from the fire that burns him
Mother holds on to the bones with screaming resolution.
"Leave it over there," he tiredly, tactlessly tastelessly tells her.
Her heart congeals as fear clashes with stubborn hope
And cathartic maternal instinct contests the arrogance of medical science
"No!" Vehemence turns to rage. "He will live!"
"I will grow him with my rage!"
The wisp bursts, the coffin falls empty, shattered into a million pieces.
And where it falls she marks the spot with her rage.
Silently, she wraps the frame, willing him to live
Breathing her own rage into him
As medical detachment angers a mother's faith
"He will live."

DEATH AT FIRST SIGHT

Mama Elsie's loud wail loads the
morning's stillness
Hushing the familiar chirping of nightingales
and crowing cocks
For death has swept across the village floor.
And brave mongrel dogs whine and whimper
Tucking frightened tails between timid legs.
Children aroused to the wailing of a belly on fire
For while everyone stirs to the kiss of the sun,
Wiping eyes tickled by its light
The broom of death sweeps hard and strong over
Mama's house,
Taking Puppa's breath, like useless cobweb in its
horrid wake.
Ice now tucks Grandpa where Mama once laid, till
he is out of sight.
A tor of ice like a dirt grave covers this
giant of a man
Stretched out in Mama's bed, emotionless,
motionless, impassive
Balminess turns to icy cold in the torrid midday sun.
The pans under his gloomy bed drip a lonely elegy,
Catching his watery wintry draught
With which we shall bathe in that numinous pan,
for our good
For Grandpa's dead water is ours too,
Death for him, but life for us lest the broom returns
To complete some business and find some
trash exposed.

THE WOMAN WHO WARNS

"Death! Death! Death!"
 Trees dare not look,
Covering their faces from her form,
Hit by the midnight moon
Immobilized by fear at the words
Coming from within her
With vitality all of their own
Ta Gwen's taut drum beats
In its raucous language
 Booming death across the frightened stones
"Prepare the calico and the board,
the hammer and the nail!"
Petrified mothers slip cautiously
Out of crocused bed to count off children,
Sleeping like gungo peas
Podded in well-ordered rows
And watch their heaving,
 Inspecting every turn,
Every dream-filled twitch for life.
Baby fathers in illicit beds,
Clear guilty throats,
Look askance at the time,
Wanting to go home.
The spirit takes her.
She stops.
She convulses to the possession
Eyes bulging
Trying hard to keep the spirit within

She beats the drum
To a thrilling crescendo
She chants a strange guttural rhythm,
In tune with the charmed shadows of the night
"Death! Death! Death!
Prepare the calico and the board, the hammer and the nail!"
A black cat envelope in the dark
Screams in pain in the indistinguishable
Nearness, again, and again.
The spirit moves within her,
She cannot contain herself.
She falls, exhausted.
The drum rolls,
The drumstick plays a melody
As it falls fighting the dusty marl road
Felina falls out of her bed, Unconscious … dead.

GUMBEH

Call Windel
Someone got hit
The plot was set and Uncle G
Walked right into it.
Call Windel
Uncle G is sick
They take his diseased infested body
Out in the midnight fire wrapped in white sheet
Call Windel
Hide the children
Spirits are offended by innocence
The spirits of Africa shall arise tonight
And make Uncle G better
Call Windell
Beat the djembe drums.
Let the rhythm of her language
Call along the dark mountains
To invite the spirits to do Windel's bidding
Call Windell,
There's a stirring
Every spirit in Africa's grave now hears
The calling drums are coming.
Call Windel
She's in myal now
The spirits have taken her over,
She's unrecognizable, dancing,
Pirouetting a nocturnal requiem.
Call Windel

Dark tension fills the air.
Uncle G is trembling in the dead white sheet,
The drums are beating faster, faster, faster
Chattering in dialects of the dead
Call Windel
Twist the chicken's neck
Its blood drenches the white sheet crimson red,
Glistening in the fierce fiery dark.
Call Windel
Pour white rum,
Blood and rum burn a frightening fire
Against Uncle G's limp body.
Call Windel

UNWANTED

Fate sent Eric to stay with Mama Enid
And Precious to stay with Miss Birdie
But me, I stayed put for nobody wanted me.
Laying listlessly, languidly,
Embracing the effervescent night
I cling to the pillow of my loneliness
Sucking my thumb in meek withdrawal
Hanging on to life by a black thread
Unseen by the dark light Wanting to live my dream
To love, to hope.
But tears scrape my discarded face
In the wretched and uneven trenches
Of life.
I create my songs,
Wordless songs of the spirit
And dance to my own tempo
And sing in the middle of the hellish night
Watching peenie-wallies
Lighting my panicked night
And push my ears against the breeze
Listening as it murmurs my name
In gossip-like undertones
For tomorrow's sun
Will strike at the darkness of tonight.

FED

Mama Enid soaked the alluring bammy thick
With oil in a protesting ashed Dutch pot,
As I scream my innocence
Unheard, for it was said I was craven
And so to quench the deep invented hunger
That tormented my jutting bones
My dusky corpulent belly
Shining murkily in the midday sun
My rib cage heaving
Like meagre canes
Hanging from a punctured tractor.
Mama was determined to temper my greed
As a black perturbing crow,
Cawing in the candid distance
She dexterously fried
A piece mackerel
A mound of salt squeezing through
Fins and gills and diamond flesh
Its perforated form
Laced in the fierce fiery fumes
Fighting for her victory over me
Gazing listlessly at me
To teach me a lesson Eat this!
Salt and mackerel and bammy
Blended and pressed
To the core of my body
Only to contort the actual
Deprivation of my soul

My imagined greed
Countenanced by this strange punishment
Wanting to bring back up
The strange concoction
To the now empty plate
For Mama did not know
The birthplace of my hunger.
So I swallowed hard.
She smiled, triumphant.

UPSIDE DOWN LOVE

Tears ran down my mom's face stained
Like browning, running on livid colourless.
Her soul crumpled in her belly
As thoughts like icepick chip at her spirit.
I stumbled over the fuming
Chair watching her contemplating
Her past, her present, and future
Wrapped up in
Regret and fear and hope.
She curses at me
"Dead Dog!"
"Johncrow!"
"Dead Carrion!"
Waves of mud
Slide over my dark soul
As I sink deeper and
Deeper into myself
A hellish hole
Becoming my comforting home.
Her tears thud against my beating heart As I ask
with confused eyes, "Why me?
What have I ever done, but love you?"
As her love grips me in her rage
Rivering angrily down her brown face
"You are as black as night."
"Your face as horrid as your father's"
"Worthless"
"Cruff"

29

"You will not come out to any good."
Her anger taunts me, jeers at me
For my father is the object of her pain
I am the product of her shame
And frustration gives way to seeping ire
And anger pitches out
Like a bucket of vomit
Upon the head of her beloved firstborn
Staining him, as she was stained
Flaying his soul with words so deep
That no guava switch could reach…
But still knowing of her uncontestable love,
That cauldron of intense fire
That stirs her everyday
To go to the Estate in the
Confronting the backbreaking sun
Till her brown skin is peeled by its inferno
Her gentle hands made callous in the
Estate's manure
Planting rows and ordered rows
Structured in a platoon of dignity
Till the row becomes of Battalion of self-respect
That she may eke out an existence of anticipation
To nourish a hungry boy
In that silent promise that she made to heaven
That, that that tied her to paradise,
Would that one day seal the deal
That her boy would come out to something.

LICE

Curled in black pepper-like grain
Or improperly planted rows of peas
My gnatted head breathes life of its own
Breeding a settlement of lice
That no Quitoso could ethnically cleanse
But Mama rocked me in her tattered lap
And I breathed her comfort
For Mama wars for my head
As she goes platoon by occupied untidy platoon
With hands trained for the battle
Scarred and scalded and bloodied
 By previous clashes between generations
Creatures so resurgent,
So fierce in their occupation
But Mama kept on fighting,
Till my rooted head surrenders sore from the battle
And scalp collapses under the onslaught
And Mama rests, retreats to return
And the lice live to fight another day

DREAM

One of the brown chairs
Taken from the dining table
Graciously acquiesces to be my headrest again
And Uncle Vincent's orange trunk
That he took with him from America
He had brought from his farm work
Filled then with America and goodies
Patiently assents to bear my reed-like frame Feet
hanging over the edge of the trunk.
Like a derisory giant in a pauper's bed
I curled like a tired purring puppy,
Pulling what slim, thin scruffy sheet I could
Over the endarkened boundaries of my soul
As there, moonlight dances
Through the cracked ceiling
And dinosaur-strength lizards croak
A beautiful cacophony
I dream of lying in the tall green grass,
Wide-eyed, drinking in the sumptuous sun
My virtuous vision took me to another place
Beyond my confused cot
A dream of another place,
Idyllic, Edenic, Rapturous,
With the smell of rich Genie floor polish
And the grandeur of "rainer pumps"
Watering plush canefields
Creating thousands upon thousands
Of celestial rainbows

As cotton white egrets soar magnificently
Calling spontaneously to each other
Wings reaching out beyond the expanse of time
Like there was no tomorrow

HANDS UP

Time stopped.
The sun turned into a fiery ball
Every sweat gland opens to wash my sins away
As Fisher's gun trained its obnoxious gaze
At my trembling heart
Ready to drink my blood
Raging in fearful frenzied fright.
Helpless hands raised heavily at his command
Lungs collapsing in flashes of lightning,
The gun threatening me with its deadly grip
Laughing luxuriously at my powerless eyes
As tears gush from them in sultry spurts
My chest heaved with
The weight of a thousand graves
For Corporal Fisher was determined to kill me.
His officer's stoic gun now
Smirking silently at attention
Waiting for a command
To spew its poisoned bullets Into my terror-drenched rags To course through my boiling veins.
I stood dead, pulse lost, heart stopped.
Fisher suddenly sheathed the monster.
I gulped.

FIRST CONTACT

"Where is my son?"
The shop piazza dances with anxiety
As I warily approach
Pulling my pride over my nakedness
Dressed with feet whitened in Holland's marl
And a piece of exhausted brown short pants That
feebly attempted to cover the pegs of my buttocks
For my father has come to see me.
Verdant cane leaves are hushed
And butterflies watch bated from a distance
The mongrel lies still,
Licking its slender wet pink tongue
Listlessly across its fly-kissed face.
Stunningly feathery white clouds unhurriedly
Paint serenity in continuity
Across the village's sky
Denzil, Gary, Blue, and Eric
Laugh excitedly, naked guts heaving in the midday
Sun
Till I'm out of sight lost in the shop
Facing my hero
My father
That unfulfilled dream about to incarnate
What a man!
Finally, face to face.
The faint shop is now garlanded
As Kilimanjaro's mountain stands with Amma
I forfend my proud eyes, for I may not look

At the form of his majesty and live
Pride and joy ooze through my soul.
"What do you want?"
Life takes on new meaning,
For divinity has spoken
To transport me beyond every harsh longing
My heart is quickened in a moment
My hunger, my thirst burn me to my nude marl kissed toes
About to be assuaged in the moment of the meeting
"A bun and a drinks!"
A carefully worded request.
Surely no God would hesitate at that submission.
But Kilimanjaro roars back
Derision displays scorn
And contempt catapults shame
"Move! Get out of here!"
Humiliation crash-lands across
My shocked blackened cheek
And Kilimanjaro transforms into Ogbunabali
And the spirits howl in knee-slapping ridicule
And the sweltering heat of the shop
Becomes a chamber of claustrophobic
Nightmare in the midday sun
I cannot breathe,
Nor bear the nauseating weight of the moment.
Tiredness drains me.
I run….

WHEN IT RAINS

Raindrops kiss my face
Gently, velvety softly
And invite me to strip
And I'm seduced down to my innocence
Laughing, and my voice ricochets satisfied against
The mystery of ecstasy
For here the sky intersects the earth
And stars run and hide,
And the sun stands back
At the supremacy of the spectacle
As raindrops pull the earth up to join the heaven,
And everything is working backwards
And all is well with the world,
I stretch out my cheerful hands
To gleefully embrace every drop
As tender diamonds fall from heaven
Enrich me with absorbing delight
Satisfying every silent yearning
 As crown and pavilion meet
 Covering ebony nakedness in splashes of light
And still, I laugh
Dancing in the romance of the moment.

FIRST LOVE

Maxine's dusky eyes dance with angelic innocence
Her thick black hair radiates with a thousand
ribbons,
Like rainbows reverberating on the village ceiling,
Her brows glow, furrowed as in deep intense
thought
Her head persuasively held to one side dazzling
magnificently.
She mastered her pencil so superbly scholarly
Statuesque in erudition at her broken desk
There emanated an unfathomable magnetism
from deep within
That made me wonder if somewhere in her
unplumbed measure
There might be a flicker of the perpetual
reciprocity of love
That may glow even faintly in my famished
direction
For love was the gift of every soul to be lit
only by another
That together the world may be warmed in love's
intensity
I reached over to look into her hallowed book,
To see prose or poetry, to be fed on the lyrics
of the angels
The author of lyrics among saged composers
But instead, I feel the stern rebuke of her
warrior pencil

Defending her dignity with intense defiance
Gouging, scorning, resenting attempted intimacy
 Blood trickles slowly and deliberately
down my arm
"Leave me alone…. You are my cousin."

ZION

Head wrapped blood-red in the traditions of the
revivalists
Coloured pencils sticking out with their secret codes
Zion stands a diminutive figure of a man,
no… a demigod
Strangely elegantly tall in the crowd of
pulsating singers
Melodic in the songs of Zion, excitedly frenzied
He walks alone, mysterious,
Possessed with the powers of the other world
For he knows who hurts whom without human lips
And he sees where the plots are planted without
human eyes And he feels the trembling joy of every
heart without touch.
The mysterious recurring trance-inducing beat of
the goat skin drums
Rattle heavy across the night sky in worship of God
Aunty Joyce's distinct melody fills the night sky
Zion comes to the house and searches out
the deep places.
With mighty spirits into dark and uncharted places,
he walks
Where owls are afraid and green lizards
dare not venture
Directing his gaze into the soul of the darkness
The sound of the drums ricochets against the night
And boomerangs back to the frenzied company
Some holding ethereal candles of varying hue

'Till Zion finds the guilty place
He stands on the spot where the plot is set,
To kill, to wound, to stifle, to set back,
To cramp and paralyze
He commands that the culpable spot be mined
And the diggers dig with sweaty passion
Till the vial is found
The frenzied crowd is ecstatic with victory
For the trap is broken and someone is free.
Now Zion can return to Roses Valley
To wait for the next call,
Another plot would soon be set.

SICK AGAIN

Lanny from Vere,
 A fiercely arrogant man
 With a paunch befitting his conceit
Would rumble in laughter
Across the village floor,
Slapping his shop counter
Till the salt fish tail
At the end of the counter Would swim away in fright
And the bun case would withdraw.
When he was without his shirt,
The angry rip from his back
Diagonally futtering across His belly
Like winged barbed wire reminded
 Everyone that Lanny was after all wretchedly sick.
The white-cloaked doctors had taken
With knives and trumpets took
A tired kidney out of him,
For he was too fat to carry it.
His body couldn't manage his weight.
He would often fall swooning
Under his own darkness
And like liquored man
In a drunken stupor
For Lanny was sick. But he knew how to laugh
and how to enjoy life.
And the petit Aunty Imo
Would silently bear his arrogance,

For she was our Aunty,
And he was only Lanny,
Lanny from Vere whom we knew was sick
And their compensated pride was well-placed
For they brought the Delco plant
And television, and electric floor-polish
And curtains and electric light
To our pristine village
But Lanny from Vere would often block out,
For he was sick.
And Aunty Imo would call Sherma and Shereen
To help her help Lanny from Vere
Who had fallen unconscious on the shop floor
Slumping helplessly over the bag of rice
And fan him back to consciousness from
medical stupor
For Lanny from Vere could not stand up
On his own weight for too long
And the strange doctors Have taken
one of his kidneys,
For he was too fat, and he was sick.
And the men of the village
Would shake their heads at the news
For this giant of a man was fallen again,
And again, and they could not diagnose
For these men were cane cutters and
Yam planters and rum drinkers who knew
The power of the sun and cerasse tea,
Who drank any poison for they knew the
power of buzzy
And they were well,
But Lanny from Vere was sick

FIGHT

Doreth stripped naked in her violent fury
Leaving on, only her tattered slip
Her upper body screams a heated sensitivity
For all, young and old alike, to gawkily soak up
As she screamed expletives in the sultry air
To fight the woman who wanted her man
For a man was a precious commodity
Worthy of any battle
The village crowded around like dogs in
mating season
To see this spectacle of gallantry as the
other woman
Easily slipped into her nothingness
Leaving wide-eyed boys gasping
In delighted heart-bursting enthralled mix-up
As the warrior woman grabbed Doreth
At the inner consultation of her thighs,
For there the village was to know
Was the peculiar place of masculine attraction -
And throws her to the gaping ground
And Doreth falls in slow motion
 Grabbing powerlessly at air
And her slip is now over her head, revealing ...
more
And the warrior woman calls her a dirty bitch,
And grabs her hair which comes out in her hand,
For Doreth's hair was a wig
And the warrior woman is thrown off balance

And tumbles to the ground atop Doreth
And together they writhe in the dark dust
And Dorerth recovers and pounds her with a rock
"Leave my man," She screams
And blood flows from the warrior woman's head
And suddenly she is limp,
As blood pumps from the cave in her head
By the dirty village standpipe,
And someone throws a pan of water in her face
She shakes her head violently
And she is alive again
And Doreth kicks her in the teeth
And the village walks away, Doreth triumphant, and goes back home
To Basil for another round of beating.

BEATING

Fist, scrubbing board, broom, slippers, guava
switch, fan belt
All formed an intimidating arsenal of weapons
Subduing wayward wanton wicked children,
For everyone knows that children are to be seen
and not heard
And to secure this momentous monumental mission,
Responsible, respectable, and righteous rule
Knew how not to spare the rod and spoil the child.
For the child is easily spoiled but the rod of
correction
No matter the size nor its constitution was not
to be spared
In bending the brutish tree while it is young
and tender
For to try later would be to break the bark
and break yourself against it.
And beating was to be administered everywhere
 and anywhere,
While having a bath in the pan outside
in the front yard
When Aunty Sis would unsuspectingly shock
your sud-soaked body
With a sudden, solid, and soundless swish of
the guava switch
Or a murderation just after you have said your
"Our Father"
 And sweetly settled in the sack, when suddenly

the fan belt
Would slither into the bed, extending Uncle
Vincent's striking arm
And startled, we would scamper like poisoned rats
under the bed,
Fearing its long inescapable sadistic reach
Or Aunty Sis telling Teacher Forrester that her yard
was disciplined
And giving the principal carte blanche to beat me
however she wished, With the one proviso: "not his
eyes nor his seed."

BAMBOO AVENUE

Luxuriant slender, excited bamboo stretch,
clasp, and embrace
In joyful amusement across the gloomy
mysterious road,
Creating three bravura tunneled miles of a verdant
conflicting canopy Arching the scenic, shadowy
roadway from Lacovia to Shaws.
The barber green is coloured with black stars,
then bright ones
As night and day play hide and seek with each other
in one moment
And the eternal breeze transports a song, hooting in
the adventurous leaves
A message of deep-held secrets, wanting to tell all,
but holding back
As green thin vegetation seals their lips, holding
their glamour high
And dried foliage drained from the excitement fall
far onto a soft brown bed
Clothing the sun-shaded floor where stringy
bamboo roots are exposed,
Brazen, without apology, for they too hold back
their blathered stories
Of lovers coalescing in the night, and of travelers
crashing to death
In the darkened eclipsed midday golden twilit
teasing sun
And tourists awed by the unique dazzle and the

creaking hush that hug
The distance, and blocks out the stars and engages the trickling sun
Till light returns at the end of the mysterious bubble and life pushes through

LOST IN THE CEMETERY

Graves whisper our names in the silence
As we frantically searched to find the track
Pushing tall colluding grass out of the way
Searching for the way home
Bumping desperately into stern tombs
And unmarked indifferent languishing crypts
"Eric, Eric, Mark, Mark, Eric, Mark"
As we look panic-struck at each other
Eyes swimming in fright,
Hearts beating a thousand deaths
Crumpling any hope of being found
For Anty Sis wanted nothing more
Than that we got an early start on our education
And Miss May Basic School was our
immortal hope
But it was beyond the cemetery
At the back of the tired village.
Black dirty graves look distrustfully at us
Taunting our reason for being there
And feet unclad sop grave dirt
And recently wreathed mounds of earth
Seem opposed to this strange intrusion
We fought with puerile fury
To free ourselves from the ordourless death
Till we see the opening of the dirty path,
We breathed, for death could not keep its prey.

FOUR ROADS

Incense burns, unfurling a ghoul-like inferno at
Four Roads
For there, suspicion, sovereignty, and séance meet
And duppy-possessed black cats meow a
humanlike hymn
And the moon pushes light out of the way,
dancing the cats' dirge.
And the headless chicken flutters in the square,
squawking
Its blood rushed like red diamond droplets to the
hungry pavement
And the piece of parchment paper burns a
shadowy fire
With names of the offended drenched, deluged
in sulphur.
Odours inundate the forbidden square for here dark
willing spirits Intersect with searching insatiate
humanity, lusting for power,
To know who had set the plot to obeah the now
death-ridden child
To send back a blow by the power of the dead to
those who offend
To stop the power of the curse that keeps Danny
from getting a farm work ticket
To find out who turned down Neville that he fails
Common Entrance again
And the fear-filled dogs howl with tails hiding
between trembling legs

And the owl flutters carrying a strange message to
the world of the dead
And rat bats sizzle in the midnight night fire,
Till the hot freezing Four Roads tremble at
its own power
And morning breaks to bathe the wretched crossing,
And children walk to the side to go to school
And mothers watch to see them safely
across the road
And still, the road is drunk, drunk with
the blood of men and ghosts.

ODE TO MISS BECKFORD

You made me stand majestic in grade one
Lofty, all-knowing, erudite
Every red hook stick glittered on my page Giving me limitless hope.
You made me believe that I could write
As you completed my fractured letters
Making my calligraphy stunning And told me that I was bright.
You left the safety of your classroom
Followed me through the craggy cane piece
Pass the boys' wrenk pit toilet
So I could point you to my house.
A puerile mob followed, glittering in the light
I was proud, shining like a diadem
I know now that you never could have seen it,
The canefields blocked your view
But you made me believe you did
And made me feel my hovel was a palace, not trite
And other picky head boys believed I was your pet
I was well placed, properly, poised.
You allowed me to sit at your desk, my place by rite
And life took me by your hand
And strolled me along till
My foundations were good
And your gentle wind blew me
To stand, to focus, to stay in the fight.

BURNING CANE

Fire crackles an orange and red blanket across
the estate sky
And a kaleidoscope of colours dances in the
cloudless night
Melding a full moon garlanded by watching excited
stars laughing
As rats and mongooses run from their
charred homes,
Once luxuriant palatial dwelling carved by
architects of nature
Consumed now by the hellish inferno
As fervent frightful heat turns
Confidence into confusion, cremating a hapless goat
In its arrogant eerie, and uncontrollable rage
Tied there wailing to a dreadful death.
Happy excited boys giggle sheepishly
As black soot kisses their black peppered heads
Anticipating the cutting that is to come
And skilled men sharpen their hungry machetes
Patiently gliding files over thirsty machetes
Eager to swing at the root of White Dog
The Estate's sweetest cane.

PINKY POND

Pinky Pond teems with fish, frogs, and beautiful
flora
Gaulins with giraffe-like necks gracefully ride cattle
drinking their fill
Duck and teels walk quickly on the pond's surface
And skimpily-clad boys throw stones and
mango seeds
Making them skip across the pond's
diamond surface
And happy girls laugh joyfully at their valiant
boyfriends' prowess
The woman of the village dressed in bra and slip
Come with wash pans skillfully set on cotter
on their heads
 Filled with dirty clothes and Fab and Blu
To keep the family clean and to catch up on the
Tasty morsels of the Village's diet.
Pinky Pond too is home, for here Anty Sis,
A ward of the State is domiciled atop with
her offspring
And children obediently get water from the pond
To wash plate and water her pride –
Her Joseph Coat and Periwinkle and Stinking Mary
and Crotons.
Time stands still, there are no clocks here atop
Pinky Pond
For there Uncle Vincent plays his record changer
And we dance to "Where did he go" and

And we listen to "Duclimena Her Life in Town,"
On our little blue radio
And play Dandy Shandy, and catch lizards and tie them out in our pastures
And when we were peckish we made pepper pot
And Mama would give us corn sham
And we would buy ice from Miss Mirrie
And Sunday Dinner would always have a tups of Dragon Stout In the carrot juice
And all would be well with the world
For Pinky Pond was our home.

CHRISTMAS MORNING

No Christmas trees lit our homes
No hope that Santa would fly by guided by Rudolph
No stockings left at night, for so they would be
found in the morning... empty
But we knew the richness of Christmas morning
We meet to sing that song
"Good Morning, Happy Christmas Morning
Neighbour show me the gangland walking
Happy Christmas Morning"
And Mass Coalin would make the goat
skin drum talk
And Miss Coolie Gyal would have the fire under
the goat soup
And Big Sil would kill a calf
And at the break of day
The Village would stir
And Everywhere was rich with the sounds at the
birth of hope
And we would start to march around the Village
First one yard, then the next
And as children, we would get one personal bottle
of aerated water
And Men would drink Bear and Dragon and
Guinness

ABOUT THE AUTHOR

Napoleon Black had his formative learning days at Miss May Basic School in Middlesex, the village that adjoined his village. After those early days, he moved on to Holland Primary School on the Holland Bamboo main road.

He is the first child of Cislyn but is not sure where in his paternal narrative he falls as a child. He met some of his paternal siblings in his teen and adult life. In fact, Napoleon will say that He is an only child who has brothers and sisters, who have brothers and sisters who are not his brothers and sisters.

He values time alone as being alone was among the defining features of his early life, and lived mainly from learning to answer his own questions as answers from the community were not satisfying and meaningful

He loved reading and would read anything he could get his hands on, and reading opened his imagination to great possibilities.

His village means a lot to him, and feels that it has taught him to value culture and humanness. In the crucible of that village, he has learned to contend with the highs and lows of life, the ups and downs of reality, and how continuity is informed by the foundation of community.

Made in the USA
Columbia, SC
01 May 2024